THE WATER BABIES

by
Charles Kingsley

Illustrated
by
Anne Grahame Johnstone

DERRYDALE BOOKS

Once upon a time there was a little chimney-sweep called Tom.
Tom couldn't read or write and he didn't care much about that. He
was always dirty because he never washed and he didn't care about
that either. What he did mind was when his master beat him every
day of his life. And when the soot got in his eyes and made them
smart and sting.

Tom's master was Mr. Grimes, the meanest, cruellest bully in
the whole land. Mr. Grimes spent all the money Tom earned for
him on himself and on tobacco for his pipe.

One day Mr. Grimes got a new customer which greatly pleased
him — especially as his new customer was Sir John of Hall Place
— a great big house in the country with so many chimneys to
sweep you couldn't count them.

And so, early the next morning, Tom and his master set out,
Grimes riding the donkey in front and Tom with the brushes
walking behind.

Tom had never been so far into the country before and longed to stop. But he did not dare. And, after a while, they caught up with a tall, handsome woman in a crimson petticoat. She had a gray shawl over her head and her eyes were bright.

"I'll walk with your boy!" she told Grimes, when he invited her to ride behind him on his donkey.

And so she did! She talked to Tom about himself until he quite lost his heart to her — not even guessing that she was a Fairy, when suddenly and without warning she vanished from sight!

When they reached the big house the gates were opened by a keeper and they were sent round to the back door.

The housekeeper came and gave Grimes orders as to what he might and might not do before taking them into a fine big room. Then, after a kick from his master which sent him into the grate, Tom started up his first chimney.

Tom stopped counting all the chimneys
he swept that morning. In the end, he
was so tired that he lost his way among
them and finally came down the wrong
one!

He found himself in a room that was
all white — white window curtains, white
bed curtains and white furniture. But it
was a little girl in the white bed that
made him gasp aloud. She was so lovely,
with her golden hair spread all over the
white pillow, that Tom could not bear to
take his eyes away from her.

At first Tom could not believe she was
real. "She must be a beautiful wax doll,"
he told himself. Then he saw her breathe!

Poor Tom! His wonder at seeing the little girl in white was suddenly changed to horror at seeing himself! For he had caught sight of himself in her long mirror. Was that dirty black ragged figure Tom, the little chimney-sweep? It must be! Tom turned away quickly, tears of shame in his eyes and with only one desire. He must escape up the chimney again before she woke up and saw him. But then the little girl opened her eyes and when she saw dirty Tom she began to scream. In rushed her old nurse and tried to grab him. But Tom was too quick for her. He was out of the open window in a flash and clambering down the spreading tree underneath.

Once free of the house
Tom took to his heels, with
the shouts of "Stop Thief!"
ringing in his ears.

"After him! After him!" shouted Sir John. And after him they went — the gardener, the keeper, the dairymaid and the groom and others besides, shouting and yelling as Tom ducked and dodged.

He ran across the park as if a pack of hounds were after him, struggling for breath, heart pounding.

Once free of the great park, he made for the woods just as any hunted animal might do. But the woods offered him no proper place to hide and the fallen branches slowed him down.

The shouts of his pursuers were growing faint as Tom left the woods for the vast lonely moors that stretched endlessly before him.

The rough bracken and
heather tore at Tom's bare feet
as he ran on. And when he could
no longer run, he slowed down to
a walk. Soon he found he was
climbing and he stopped every
now and then to draw breath.

"I'm free of them at last," he
told himself. "They will never
catch me now."

And all the time he was
climbing he had no idea that not
far behind was the Fairy he had
lost his heart to early that
morning.

"If only I had something to
eat," he thought, "I could keep
on forever and ever."

Now Tom's poor head was starting to spin and he began to imagine that he could hear the sound of church bells ringing a long, long way off. "If there is a church — there should be people" he said to himself. "And it is people I need — or just one kind person to give me shelter and something to eat and some water to drink."

He was certain he had long ago lost his pursuers. He was certain, too, that now he could never go back. He had seen the last of his cruel master that morning. Never again would he be the poor little chimney-sweep working for Grimes!

But when you have reached the top of the mountain there is nowhere to go but to begin climbing down. And bravely, Tom set out to do just that. Below, he could see a deep green valley and woods — and through the woods a clear silver stream. Tom longed to reach the stream and put his hot sore feet in its cool water.

The valley, the woods and the stream looked a hundred miles away to Tom as he began the long, dangerous climb down. And when he found himself on top of a high cliff, he hung there for a moment. Then, glancing downwards over his shoulder, he thought he spied a little cottage set in a garden. And his friend in the crimson petticoat!

For Tom there was now no turning back and he was terribly tired and dizzy by the time he reached the valley. So he lay down on the grass and fell fast asleep. After a while, he opened his eyes, got up, and stumbled away along a narrow path that led to the prettiest cottage in the world.

The door was open and Tom peeped into the room, too shy to enter. In a high-backed chair sat an old woman with a black silk handkerchief tied over her clean white cap — and at her feet an old ginger cat.

"That old lady must be a teacher of sorts," Tom decided, seeing that opposite her on wooden benches sat two rows of well-scrubbed children.

All the clean, rosy children saw Tom and began to stare at his dirty, black figure. Some of the boys started to laugh and some of the little girls looked frightened.

"Who are you and what do you want?" cried the old woman.

And when poor Tom remained silent, she cried again: "I can see what you are! You are a sweep! Go away! I don't want any chimney-sweeps here!"

"I only want a drink of water," Tom said weakly.

"You can get water in the stream," returned the woman sharply. "Off with you!"

"But I — I can't get there," Tom protested. "I'm too hungry and thirsty to take another step!" And he sank down on the doorstep.

Then the old lady looked at him more closely through her eye glasses. "The boy is sick," she declared at last. And she got up and went over to him. "I'll not give you water," she went on. "I'll give you milk. That will be better for you!"

The children were silent now. And the boys stopped laughing at Tom as their teacher went off to get the milk and some bread.

As soon as Tom had drunk the milk he began to look better and more like himself.

But when he tried to get up he was so
faint that the old lady had to help him to
his feet. She led him to the barn outside,
saying, "Rest on the hay and when school
is over I'll come back." Then she went
away expecting Tom to fall asleep.

Tom did not fall asleep after all. He tossed and turned on the soft sweet hay, his heart filled with longing for the cool waters of the river. Then, only half-asleep, he began thinking of the beautiful little girl in the wonderful white room and how he had terrified her because he was so dirty. And he began to wish that he was clean. "I must be clean," he told himself. "I must wash in the river."

How he got into the meadow, Tom had no idea. But, all of a sudden he was there with the stream just in front of him. And he dipped his hand in the water and found it cool and refreshing. So he pulled off all his old rags quickly and put his hot feet into the water. Into the river he went, deeper and deeper.

And all this time he had no idea that the Fairy was there — at first behind him as he left the barn, and then in front of him. She entered the river before he did and her crimson petticoat floated away from her and the white water-lilies floated round her head.

Then all the water-fairies came to give her a royal welcome home. They took her away to the bottom of the river rejoicing that their Queen was back amongst them once again.

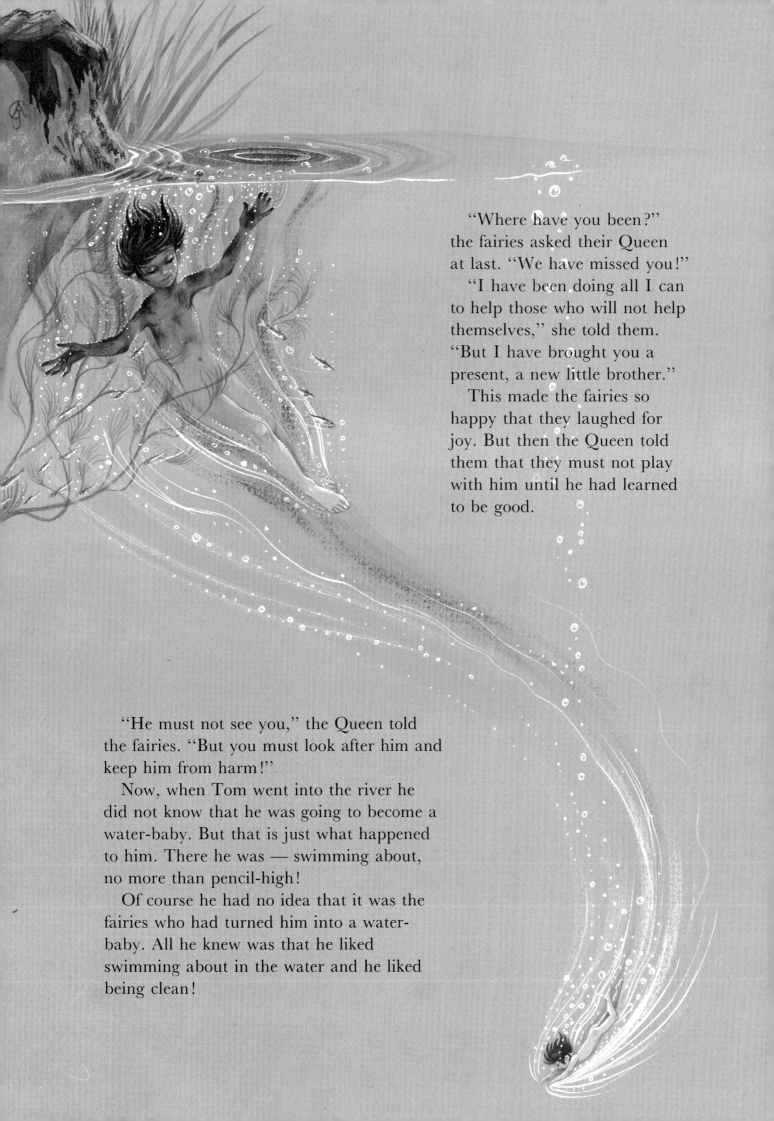

"Where have you been?" the fairies asked their Queen at last. "We have missed you!"

"I have been doing all I can to help those who will not help themselves," she told them. "But I have brought you a present, a new little brother."

This made the fairies so happy that they laughed for joy. But then the Queen told them that they must not play with him until he had learned to be good.

"He must not see you," the Queen told the fairies. "But you must look after him and keep him from harm!"

Now, when Tom went into the river he did not know that he was going to become a water-baby. But that is just what happened to him. There he was — swimming about, no more than pencil-high!

Of course he had no idea that it was the fairies who had turned him into a water-baby. All he knew was that he liked swimming about in the water and he liked being clean!

At first Tom was very happy being a
water-baby. There were so many strange
creatures to watch or tease or chase. In
the water-forest some of the oddest were
the water-monkeys and the water-
squirrels — all with six legs!

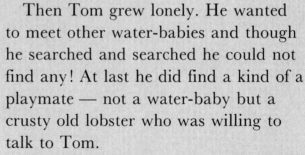

Then Tom grew lonely. He wanted
to meet other water-babies and though
he searched and searched he could not
find any! At last he did find a kind of a
playmate — not a water-baby but a
crusty old lobster who was willing to
talk to Tom.

"I wish I could find a water-baby,"
Tom confided in him, as they sat in a
hole in the rocks. "I mean to go on
looking until I do."

Poor Tom! The fairies and water-
babies were all round him but he was
not allowed to see them!

So Tom went on searching for water-babies and, as he
swam up and down, he met with an adventure which nearly
put an end to him! It all began when he found himself among
some rocks.

Do you remember the little girl in the white room? Her
name was Ellie. And, one day, Ellie and an old professor, who
was staying with her father, were exploring the rocks. The old
professor was fishing with his net under the weeds hoping to
catch something strange and pretty to show little Ellie.
Instead, he caught poor Tom! Tom got the fright of his life.
But when the professor began prodding him, his fright turned
to rage and he bit the old man's finger! And, very much
annoyed, the professor dropped him on the weeds, and Tom
dove into the water and was gone in a flash!

After his narrow escape, Tom did come across a real live water-baby and helped him plant the prettiest rock-garden of sea-weeds and anemones you have ever seen. As a reward, the fairies allowed him to meet the other water-babies.

"You must be good all the time," they warned him. "We hear Mrs. Bedonebyasyoudid is coming on Friday."

Early on Friday morning, Mrs. Bedonebyasyoudid arrived. She had a black bonnet and a black shawl and a pair of huge green spectacles on her long hooked nose. When all the water-babies were lined up in front of her she gave them sea-cake and sea-toffee and other nice things out of her basket. But when it was Tom's turn to stand before her — instead of giving him a delicious sea-cake, she popped a nasty cold hard pebble into his mouth!

Tom did try hard after that and
when on Sunday a pretty lady
called Mrs. Doasyouwouldbedoneby
came, he danced round her with
the others. And she took him in
her arms and cuddled him. Then
Tom told her that he had never
been cuddled before.

"I really will be good," he
promised. "I will!"

And for a while Tom did try.
But, sad to say, all he could think
about were sea-cakes and sea-
toffees and all the other nice
things locked away in the
cupboard that belonged to
Mrs. Bedonebyasyoudid!

One night, when everybody was
asleep, Tom crept away among
the rocks to find the cupboard.

And when he found it, the doors were open
and he thought he might just taste one of the
nice things. But after he had eaten one, he ate
another and another — gobbling everything up
as fast as he could!

And though he did not know it, all the time
and close behind him was that strange fairy
Mrs. Bedonebyasyoudid!

The fairy did not grab him or shake him.
She just looked at him sadly. And on Sunday
when kind, pretty Mrs. Doasyouwouldbedoneby
came, she said nothing either. But when Tom
asked her for a cuddle, she shook her head:

"I can't," she said, "for you are covered all
over with prickles!"

For a whole week poor Tom was very miserable. "Will you take away my horrid prickles?" he asked the old fairy when next he saw her.

"I cannot do that," said the fairy. "But I will bring you a teacher who will teach you how to get rid of them."
Can you guess who she brought? It was the little girl in white — little Ellie!

Tom's new teacher came every day of the week except Sundays, when one of the fairies took her home. And after she had been giving Tom lessons for some weeks, he began losing his prickles and Ellie suddenly recognized her pupil as the little chimney-sweep who had come down the chimney into her room.

"I know you!" she cried. "You are the chimney-sweep!"

"And I know you!" cried Tom. "You are the little girl in the white bed in the white room!" And he laughed aloud.

And then they began telling each other about themselves and Ellie explained how she had fallen off a rock into the water and the fairies had brought her to Tom. And Tom longed to give her a hug and a kiss — only he did not dare!

One day Mrs. Bedonebyasyoudid told Tom that the time had come for him to go away by himself and see the world. And brave Tom cried eagerly: "I'll go this very minute!"

"You must journey to Shiny Wall," said the fairy, "for there you will find wise old Mother Carey. She is the only one who can direct you to the Other-End-of-Nowhere."

"What shall I find there?" Tom asked.

"Your old master, Mr. Grimes," was the answer.

So Tom set out on his adventures and he had so many that they would fill another book if they were all written down.

Perhaps the best one of all was when he came upon a lively little dog that had been shipwrecked. The dog sneezed himself into a water-dog so that he could follow Tom!

But it was some strange jolly birds called mollymocks who finally took Tom and his dog as far as Shiny Wall.

"Dive under the ice floe," they told him. "When you come up again, you will be in Mother Carey's pool." And Tom, not a bit frightened, did just that!

What a large, peaceful pool Tom and his little dog found themselves in! Far away he could see the towering ice cliffs, but of Mother Carey there was no sign. Then he saw that a tall, peaked iceberg was Mother Carey herself! There she sat, without moving, chin resting on one hand, looking down at the millions of new-born creatures she had made out of the sea-water. As soon as she saw him she asked what he wanted.

"I am looking for Mr. Grimes, the chimney-sweep," he told her. "But it is taking a long time to find him."

"You will find him soon," said Mother Carey. "But don't go yet. Stay and talk to me for it is many years since I had a visit from a water-baby."

So Tom stayed and talked to the white marble lady who was as old as the world itself. And she, in her turn, told him wonderful stories before sending him on his way.

There is no use pretending that Tom had an easy task finding
Mr. Grimes. And when he did, he was very sad to see what a
state his old master was in. There he was — sticking out of the
top of a chimney, his head and shoulders just showing. He was
guarded by a fierce truncheon which kept hitting him whenever
he grumbled about his unlit pipe.

"I'm glad I found you," Tom began timidly. "You fell in the
river, didn't you? And the fairies found you? I expect they could
have changed you into a water-baby if they had wanted to."

At this Mr. Grimes grunted, supposing that Tom had come to
laugh at him. But, of course, he was quite wrong.

"I do wish I could help you," Tom went on earnestly. And at
this, Mr. Grimes began to splutter and cry real tears!

Tom took Mr. Grimes to the fairies and they took pity on him.
They sent him to sweep the ashes out of one of the craters which
was, after all, much better than being stuck fast in a great, tall
chimney!

How long Tom had been away on his travels it is hard to say. But in all that time he had not forgotten Ellie! And when he saw her again, he thought she was even more beautiful than before.

"You have grown," said Ellie.
"And so have you!" said Tom. "One day I'll be a proper man and we'll get married!"
I expect that is just what happened, don't you?